W9-DAK-738

WANDA & WINKY

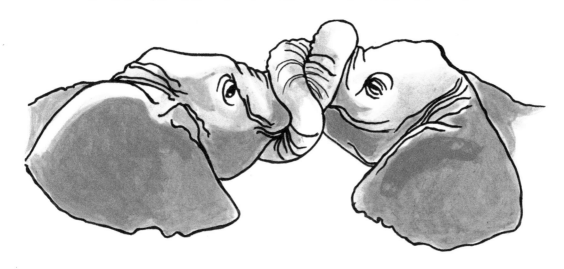

BY

LINDA K. MCLEAN

ILLUSTRATED BY

SUSAN VANDEVENTER WARNER

By the Creek Publications
Commerce Twp., Michigan
2016

DEDICATION

I dedicate this book to Ron Kagan, Executive Director of the Detroit Zoo and to Pat Derby and Ed Stewart, co-founders of the Performing Animal Welfare Society

For my grandchildren, may we only see elephants in the wild forever more.

© Linda K McLean 2016

Wanda & Winky
Copyright © 2016 by Linda K. McLean. All rights reserved.
First Edition: June 2016

ISBN: 978-0-9974810-0-6
Library of Congress Control Number: 2016942758

Editor: Mariah Fredericks
Cover and Formatting: Streetlight Graphics

No part of this book may be reproduced, scanned, or distributed in any printed or electronic form without permission. Please do not participate in or encourage piracy of copyrighted materials in violation of the author's rights. Thank you for respecting the hard work of this author..

PREFACE

This poetic work tells the story of Wanda and Winky, two Asian elephants who were captured and taken from their families as babies. They were sold by animal dealers to a zoo and to a circus. They left the Detroit Zoo in 2005 and were sent to live out their days at the ARK 2000 Elephant Sanctuary in San Andreas, CA.

That year, when I heard that Wanda and Winky would be leaving the Detroit Zoo and given their freedom, I knew I would write their story one day. I celebrated their release. I felt in my heart, "Good for you girls. Now go have a nice life!"

As I proceeded with the research of Wanda and Winky's background, I became aware of startling information about the life that elephants live while in captivity. In the back of this book, I have listed many resources that will provide you with facts that are important for you to know. It can be heartbreaking if you have a love of animals. This story, however, is meant to be uplifting and positive. And so I bid you, happy reading of a tale of two elephants who made it home.

This work is meant for children ages 5-12

In the elephant house at the Detroit Zoo,
Lived Wanda and Winky who were friends through and through.
They were beautiful animals, friendly and fun.
Gentle gray beasts that weighed nearly three ton.

Their stories began in lands faraway.
They were captured as babies and taken away.
From their home and their family they had to part.
Surely each suffered a sad, broken heart.

The elephant babies each went their own way.
A zoo, and a circus is where they would stay.
In the zoo Winky lived a life behind bars,
While Wanda was living with old circus stars.

5

ELEPHANT TALK

Our story elephants, Wanda and Winky, lived very different lives before they met each other at the Detroit Zoo. Winky was born in 1952 in the Asian country of Cambodia.

Captured as a baby, she was taken from her mother and family.

An animal dealer sold her to the Sacramento Zoo.

Wanda was born in India in 1958 and was also taken as a baby from her family.

She was sold to circuses and to zoos.

In the 1800s, elephants had become a popular attraction for circuses and zoos.

Animal dealers made a lot of money kidnapping and selling them.

Today, many circuses and zoos are releasing their elephants to sanctuaries,

Some zoos, however, continue to bring elephants to their exhibits.

At the zoo, Winky lived with her companion named Sue.

They were put on display for the humans to view.

The exotic elephants were intriguing and rare.

Winky and Sue were a popular pair.

Wanda's new owners sold her off to
A farm and a circus, a ranch and a zoo.
She moved seven times in thirty-four years.
I wonder if Wanda shed many tears.

ELEPHANT TALK

The Sacramento Union Newspaper helped raise money to buy the Sacramento Zoo an elephant. That is how "Sue" came to be and how she got her name: the Sacramento Union Elephant.

In 1955, Winky joined Sue, and they lived together for over thirty-three years.

When Sue died in 1988, the Sacramento Zoo knew it was not good for an elephant to live alone. In 1991, they sent her to live in a new place, the Detroit Zoo.

Wanda's life was more complicated than Winky's. She began her life in captivity at Disneyland, where she was called "Annette" for awhile.

She was only a baby when she moved from the Jungleland Thousand Oaks Animal Farm in California to the Carson & Barnes Circus in 1963.

She was in the circus sideshow where it was common for baby elephants to give rides.

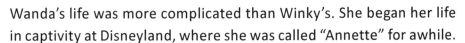

One year later, in 1964, Wanda was sold to the Kilroy Ranch where she met a new elephant friend, Missy.

Missy and Wanda were companions for thirty-three years, living together in three different zoos until Missy died in 1997.

In 1999, Wanda was sent to Detroit where she met Winky.

Their stories continue as each made their way
To the Detroit Zoo where for years they would stay.
To see Wanda and Winky was quite a delight,
This dynamic duo was a truly rare sight.

Thousands of fans came to see these two creatures.
Their tall legs and long trunks were uncommon features.
In summer they enjoyed their time in the sun,
Finding some space to play and to run.

But in Fall and in Winter their home was too cold,
Too small a space for the pair to grow old.
The hardened cement and the frozen ground,
Were painful for an elephant stomping around.

The Zookeeper said, "This is really not fair,"
They don't have a coat and their feet are quite bare.
So he sent them to live in a place far away,
Where they would have acres to frolic and play.

Some folks would grumble, "You can't send them away.
The zoo is the place where they need to stay."
But the zoo man said, "No, this is what we must do,
Wanda and Winky must not live in a zoo."

They packed up their trunks and headed out west
To a place they were sure would be only the best.
The zookeepers bid them a fond adieu.
Then Wanda and Winky left the Detroit Zoo.

ELEPHANT TALK

After decades of pleasing crowds in circuses and other zoos, Wanda and Winky came together at the Detroit Zoo in 1999.

They bonded and became close companions.

Even though it was not the hard life of the circus, they still lived in captivity and in a cold environment for part of the year.

When Wanda and Winky lived at the zoo, they had space

that was very limited compared to living in the wild where elephants can travel up to 30 miles a day.

Elephants are not used to living in cold weather, and they often suffer from arthritis and foot problems.

They traveled by truck for many a day,
Over 2,000 miles to the place they would stay.
To the PAWS Sanctuary, Wanda and Winky were sent,
Where everyone was sure they would be quite content.

ELEPHANT TALK

In April, 2005, the Detroit Zoo's Executive Director, Ron Kagan, made the decision to move Wanda and Winky to the PAWS (Performing Animals Welfare Society) ARK 2000 Sanctuary. The Detroit Zoo was the first one in the country to voluntarily give up their elephants for humane reasons.

They were given more space and freedom to live in a warmer climate.

It was heavenly!

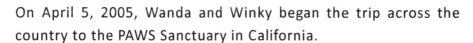

On April 5, 2005, Wanda and Winky began the trip across the country to the PAWS Sanctuary in California.

They were moved in a heated semi-truck that was specially designed for moving elephants. There was a padded floor for comfort and video cameras so the keepers could make sure they were safe.

The elephants practiced for weeks on how to get into the right compartment in the truck. Winky went in first and stood in the front. Wanda went in second and stayed in the back.

They were rewarded with their favorite treats to help them remember what to do.

Their new habitat was sunny and warm.

Wanda and Winky would come to no harm.

They could run in the grass and play in the sand.

Does an elephant smile when she's feeling so grand?

Their elephant friends welcomed them in
To a kind, loving family, their new next of kin.
The trumpets and rumbles could be heard for miles,
The elephants' happiness brought many smiles.

ELEPHANT TALK

At ARK 2000, elephants have over 100 acres of natural habitat in which to live.

They were free to roam, to play, and to graze.

These activities help them develop muscles that they were not using while living at zoos and in circuses. PAWS was founded by Pat Derby, a former Hollywood animal trainer and her partner Ed Stewart.

The PAWS Sanctuary's goals are to protect endangered animals according to the Animal Welfare Act.

On the PAWS website, you can find a biography of all the elephants who have lived there, past and present. Wanda and Winky are kind of famous!

www.pawsweb.org

Wanda began her new life with great joy,
But Winky decided to be a bit coy.
She hung out with the handlers, they were friendly and kind.
They really helped Winky relax and unwind.

Wanda was friendly, she joined in the fun,
And she basked in the warm California sun.
When Gypsy showed up, an old circus gal,
Wanda was thrilled with her new pachyderm pal.

ELEPHANT TALK

Winky felt shy when she arrived at the ARK.

She did not hang out with the rest of the herd.

She just enjoyed the sunshine and never went far from the barn.

Winky enjoyed a lot of attention and treats when she stayed near to her handlers.

Elephants are smarter than people think they are!

Wanda happily began exploring the new habitat and joined the other elephants.

On Gypsy's first trip to the elephant habitat, she was drawn to Wanda, as if she were seeing an old friend. Wanda and Gypsy had both been circus elephants and they shared a special bond when they met each other in 2009.

They became inseparable for the rest of their time together.

Gypsy had been with the Hawthorne Circus, and Wanda had been with Carson & Barnes Circus.

Perhaps they had met before while traveling with their circus shows.

Though Wanda and Winky each lived their own way,
Their new handlers loved them more every day.
Elephants happy with their new way of life,
Enjoyed plenty of space and truly no strife.

The elephant duo grew older together
Enjoying the climate of warm sunny weather.
Two friends side by side 'til the end of their days,
They taught us the beauty of elephant ways.

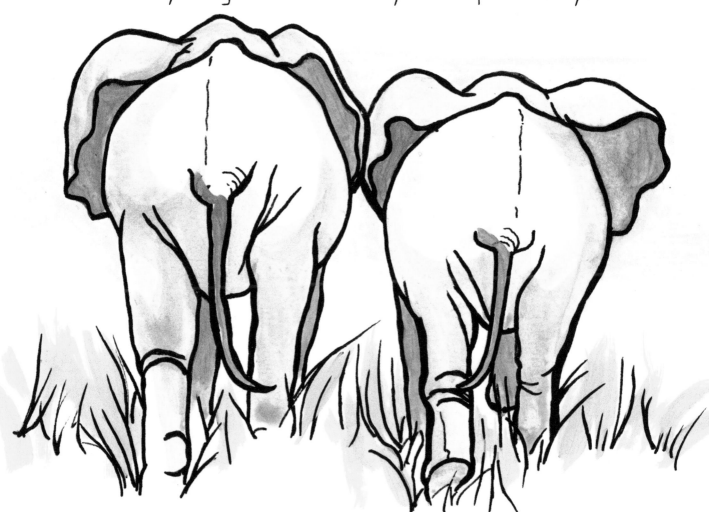

Wanda - 2015 - Age 57 Winky - 2008 - Age 56

ELEPHANT TALK

Wanda and Winky lived out their lives in peace and tranquility thanks to Detroit Zoo Director Ron Kagan's courageous act to move them to the PAWS Sanctuary. The sanctuary was a safe haven for the pair and a place where they found a new herd of pachyderms to call "family."

Winky remained free at the PAWS Sanctuary from 2005 until her passing in 2008.

Wanda enjoyed her life with friend Gypsy by her side until she passed in 2015.

I hope you enjoyed learning all about Wanda and Winky.

Why not learn more about elephants from the back pages of this book?

Perhaps you will want to get involved with one of the elephant sanctuaries.

COOL STUFF
ABOUT ELEPHANTS

 An Elephant Never Forgets is a phrase often said about elephants and it's true! Elephants have memories that can last for decades. They remember friends as well as those who may have mistreated them during their years in captivity.

 Elephants live in **herds** which are large groups of related females and their young. They are led by the oldest and largest female known as the **Matriarch.**

 Male Elephants leave the herd between the ages of 13 and 15 to live on their own or with another male.

 Elephants are **herbivores,** eating up to 400 pounds per day of grasses, leaves, shoots, roots, bamboo, and other vegetation.

 Asian elephants are an endangered species. Their population has fallen significantly over the past several generations due to habitat loss, as well as the illegal poaching of their ivory tusks.

 The Life expectancy of an elephant is 70 years in the wild, and much shorter if held in captivity due to obesity, poor health, and the stress of circus or zoo life.

 An elephant's gestation period is 22 months. Babies weigh between 200 – 250 pounds.

 The two types of elephants are Asian, which are found throughout India, China, and much of Southeast Asia, and **African** elephants who live in sub-Saharan Africa. Asian elephants have smaller ears, four nails on each foot, and different shaped heads than the African elephant. The African elephant has large ears, a different trunk, and three nails on each foot.

 Elephants have sharp hearing and they communicate through many different sounds such as trumpets and rumbles. African elephants produce 25 different calls that are unique to the human ear.

 Elephant Trunks have 40,000 muscles. Trunks are used for smelling, communicating, spraying, tearing down trees and for getting food into the mouth.

SOURCES:

Elephant World
http://www.elephant-world.com

Defenders of Wildlife
http://www.defenders.org/elephant/basic-facts

About.com – Elephants in Captivity
http://ecology.about.com/od/Ecology/fl/Elephants-What-Do-They-Eat-Where-Do-They-Live-and-What-Makes-Them-Special.htm

U.S. Fish & Wildlife – International Affairs Asian Elephants
http://www.fws.gov/international/animals/asian-elephants.html

Bradley, Carol. Last Chain on Billie: How One Extraordinary Elephant Escaped the Big Top.
First ed. New York: St. Martin's, 2014. Print.

McClung, Robert M., and Marilyn Janovitz. America's First Elephant.
New York: Morrow Junior, 1991. Print.

How to Love an Elephant

Elephants are amazingly social, intelligent, and emotional animals. They need to live with other elephants in order to have a normal life.

 If you become aware of a local circus or a small zoo that has just one elephant in its animal performance group, please petition local authorities to ban this cruel practice. Write a letter to your local newspaper editors and call the local TV news station to explain the situation.

Elephants are often trained to perform by the use of bull hooks. The use of this implement inflicts pain on an elephant's most sensitive body parts in order to train an elephant to comply with the trainer's commands.

 Bull hooks are steel poker rods with pointed ends, designed to inflict pain. You can find more information at the following website: http://www.helpphillyzooelephants.com/aboutbullhooks.html

Elephant sanctuaries are located in the United States as well as in Asia and Africa. Find out about these places and see how you can support them.

 PAWS – Performing Animals Welfare Society www.pawsweb.org

 Amboseli Trust for Elephants https://www.elephanttrust.org/

 The Elephant Sanctuary in Tennessee https://www.elephants.com

 Elephant Sanctuary South Africa http://www.elephantsanctuary.co.za/

 Riddle's Elephant and Wildlife Sanctuary http://elephantsanctuary.org/

 Two Tails Ranch http://allaboutelephants.com/

 Boon Lott's Elephant Sanctuary http://www.blesele.org/

 Elephant Nature Park http://www.elephantnaturepark.org

"Elephants are Dying Out in America's Zoos." Michael J. Berens, The Seattle Times, December 1, 2012,. http://old.seattletimes.com/html/nationworld/2019808167_elephants

"Why the U.S. Is Allowing Zoos to Import Wild Elephants From Africa." Christina Russo, National Geographic, February 18, 2016. http://news.nationalgeographic.com/2016/02/160218-elephants-zoos-swaziland-cites-fish-and-wildlife-service/

ACKNOWLEDGEMENTS

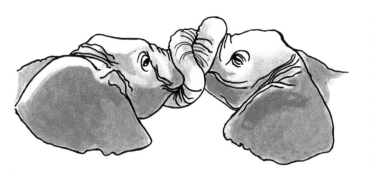

First and foremost, I want to thank the Detroit Zoological Society Executive Director, Ron Kagan, for his courageous act of sending Wanda and Winky to the PAWS Sanctuary in 2005. His actions were heartwarming and without him, there would be no story. Additionally, thanks to the PAWS Sanctuary in San Andreas, California for the operation of the facility that gives shelter and love to former exotic trade and performing animals.

One dollar from every book sold will be donated to the PAWS Sanctuary for the care and feeding of their elephants.

I would also like to thank the many people who read the story, edited, designed, illustrated, and encouraged me in so many ways. Specifically the following people deserve my gratitude:

Susan VanDeventer Warner, for her warm and charming illustrations of the journey of Wanda and Winky

Mariah Fredericks, Editor, whose words of wisdom were immeasurably valuable

Glendon Haddix, Streetlight Graphics, a talented book designer

PAWS Sanctuary for the use of Wanda and Winky photographs

Sacramento Zoo personnel for clarifying Winky's transfer to the Detroit Zoo

Kate McLean, for reading, re-reading, suggesting, and encouraging the telling of this story

Carol Trembath, friend and fellow author, for being a sounding board and for ideas that propelled the completion of the book

Glenn Miller, photographer and childhood friend, for the beautiful African Elephant photo that served as an inspiration for my commitment to telling the elephants' story.

Sarah Mellen, for her inspiring poem.

ABOUT THE AUTHOR

Linda K. McLean is a retired teacher and library media specialist with 40 years of experience in the field of education. She is the mother of three adult children and the G-ma of nine grandchildren. Among her published works are: *A Parents' Guide to Family Learning Experiences in Detroit*, printed by Detroit Public Schools and distributed to parents in 1977. *Reading Buddies Bloom,* Continental Press, 1997, and *The Heidelberg Project – A Street of Dreams,* Nelson Publishing and Marketing, 2007.

Ms. McLean enjoys writing about real events and real stories from her life. Other books in the works are a gymnastics journal, stories about Casey, her dog, and stories about the children she visited in an orphanage in Ayacuho, Peru.

Other interests of Ms. McLean's are reading, volunteer work, sports activities, musical singing groups, and creating art work of all kinds. A particular area of interest is to paint Little Free Libraries and place them in her community for the purpose of sharing free books for all.

Ms. McLean is dedicated to her family and enjoys all of the fun gatherings they have together.

ABOUT THE ILLUSTRATOR

Susan VanDeventer Warner, was born in Detroit where she developed the foundation of her artistic talent. A lifelong love of art and color has taken her on diverse paths, always including drawing, painting and design.

Included are teaching, cartooning, painting, collage, tile, space, and color design consultation. Book Illustration has been a goal and is now a new adventure for her.

Married to Norm Thompson, a Musician/ Photographer. They are enjoying their mutual love of the arts.

She is a Mother of four and Grandmother of eight.

PERFORMING ANIMAL WELFARE SOCIETY -- PAWS

www.pawsweb.org

Photo Courtesy of PAWS

*One dollar from every book sold will be donated to the PAWS Sanctuary in San Andreas, California for the support of their elephant population there. I hope you may consider lending your support to them as well, or any other elephant sanctuary that I have noted in this book.

You taught me to be gentle with nature,

To give it respect.

You taught me to care for,

Encourage, protect.

To honor life, no matter how small,

From the tiniest seed

To the vines growing tall.

Imagination, compassion,

And love was the game.

Congratulations! An elephant

Has been adopted in your name!

Thank you to Sarah Mellen, for sharing her birthday poem, written for her mom.